Under the Bed

For Teddy

A. F.

For Dad

M. R.

EGMONT
We bring stories to life

Book Band: Purple

First published in Great Britain 2015
This Reading Ladder edition published 2016
by Egmont UK Limited
The Yellow Building, 1 Nicholas Road, London W11 4AN
Text copyright © Anne Fine 2015
Illustrations copyright © Matt Robertson 2015
The author and illustrator have asserted their moral rights
ISBN 978 1 4052 8220 8
www.egmont.co.uk
A CIP catalogue record for this title is available from the British Library.
Printed in Singapore
58132/2

Series consultant: Nikki Gamble

MIX
Paper
FSC FSC® C018306

Under the Bed

Anne Fine

Illustrated by
Matt Robertson

Reading Ladder

I get scared every night.
I'm fine if Dad is in
my room, finishing my
bedtime story. 'And then
they all lived happily
ever after.'

I'm happy if Mum's there,
closing the lid of my toy
box and saying, 'Toby,
are you sure you
cleaned your teeth?'

I'm okay if Nana is sitting on the bed,
singing our bedtime song:
  'Night, night, sleep tight.
  Hope the fleas don't bite.'

And I'm all right if my brother Harry
is peeping round the door to tell me the
latest score. 'Hey, Toby! Chelsea are up
two nil!'

But after they've gone, I get scared.
I know it's silly, but I start to think there
might be something under my bed.

Something that slithers . . .

Something that creeps . . .

Something that sucks . . .

Or bites . . .

I try to tell myself it isn't true.
There's nothing there. There's never
been anything scary under the bed
since I was born. There never will be
anything scary, even if I sleep in this
bed until I'm so old I grow a beard.
And there is nothing scary now.

I really believe that. I keep believing it for about five minutes.

Then I get less sure. (Did I hear something slither? Can I hear something creep?)

Then a little bit more less sure.

(Was that a sucking noise? Do I
hear clicking teeth?)

In the end, I get so worried that
all I can do is lie still and listen
hard. I keep my eyes open in
case something scary comes out.

So I can't sleep. No one can sleep
if they are listening hard and forcing
their eyes to stay open. No one can
sleep if they are worrying about what's
under the bed.

That's when I call
them up. 'Da-ad!
Mu-um! Na-na!
Har-ry!'

In the end Dad puts his
head around the door.
He isn't very pleased.
'Oh, Toby! Why
            haven't you
                gone to
                    sleep?'

'I can't,' I tell him. 'I think there might be something under the bed.'

Dad sighs. 'What? Apart from your jigsaws? And your box of model cars? Your paints? And all your old drawings from when you were back in nursery? And your snow boots? And Harry's old trumpet? And the chocolate rabbit you're saving for a special day? And –'

I interrupt the list.

'Yes,' I say. 'Apart from my jigsaws
and cars and paints and drawings and
boots and Harry's old trumpet and
the chocolate rabbit I'm saving for a
special day. Something else.
Something horrible
and scary.'

Dad gets down on his hands and knees and looks under the bed. 'There's nothing horrible and scary there.'

'You're sure?'

'Of course I'm sure.'

'Did you look properly?'

'Yes, I looked properly!' He smiles.

I try to be brave. 'All right, then. You can go downstairs again.'

'And thank you for coming up,

Daddy,' he prompts me.

'And thank you for coming up,' I say.

He winks at me and off he goes.

I lie there for a while, feeling a little safer. But not for long. I know I can hear something rustling under the bed.

Maybe whatever it is was curled up in one of my jigsaw boxes. Waiting.

Just waiting . . .

Before I can stop myself, I've called
out again. 'Da-ad! Mu-um! Na-na!
Har-ry!'

This time it's Mum that comes.

She doesn't come in. She stands in
the doorway and tells me a bit crossly,
'Toby, you're being really silly!'

'I know,' I say. 'I know there's nothing
there. But please just take a look.'

'This is the very last time . . .!' she
warns me. But she does get down on
her knees and lift the bedcovers.

'All I can see is –'

'I know!' I interrupt her. 'Jigsaws and
cars and paints and drawings and
snow boots and Harry's old trumpet
and the chocolate rabbit I'm saving for
a special day.'

'That's right.'

'And nothing horrible and scary?'
I just ask to be sure.

'No. Nothing horrible and scary. There
never is anything scary. It's just your
imagination. So close your eyes, stop
bothering everyone, and go to sleep!'

I try. I really try. But I just know that out of the corner of my eye I saw the very tail end of something slither out from under the radiator and across the rug to hide under the bed.

I have to call again. 'Da-ad! Mu-um! Na-na! Har-ry!'

This time, it's Nana. 'You're getting far too old to fret about monsters under the bed,' she tells me firmly. 'And I am far too old to keep coming upstairs to look for them.'

'Just this once,' I say. 'I promise I won't call again.'

'You'd better not! I need my beauty sleep!' she says. But she gets down on her knees and takes a peep under the bed.

'A bit of dust here and there. Some fluff balls. A bit of dried up orange juice. But mostly it's just –'

I chant it along with her: 'Jigsaws and model cars and paints and drawings and snow boots and Harry's old trumpet and the chocolate rabbit I'm saving for a special day.'

'That's right,' she says. And she goes off downstairs.

Next time I call, I know it's Harry coming up the stairs because he makes his ghost noise.

WOOOOOO
WOOOOOO

I hear him going into his room, so when I see the strange white shape loom round my door, I know it's only Harry with his pillowcase pulled over his head. He's just trying to scare me worse.

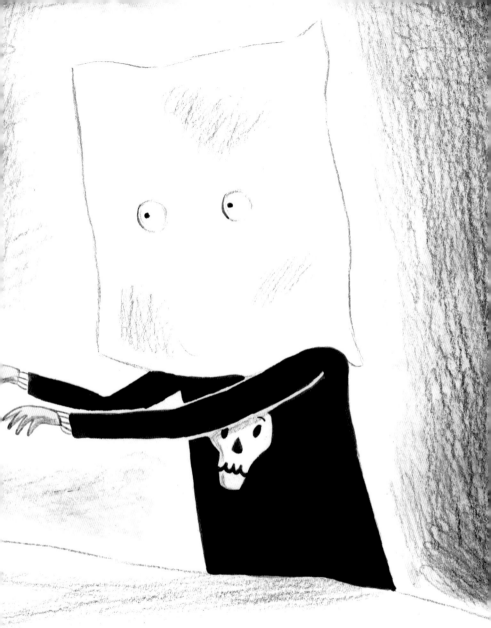

'Stop it!' I shout at him. 'This is not a joke!'

He pulls off the pillowcase. 'It is,' he says. 'A real joke. Someone as old as you worrying about scary things under the bed!'

'I'm nowhere near as old as you!'
I tell him. (Harry is three whole years
older than me. That's why he stays up
later.)

He takes a look for me. 'There's
nothing here. Just jigsaws and –'

'That's okay,' I say quickly. 'I know
that stuff.'

So Harry goes back downstairs.
And me? I lie there worrying until
I call again.

31

At breakfast, all of us had dark
shadows round our eyes. We were all
yawning. Nobody had had enough
sleep.

'This has to stop,' said Mum. 'We can't go on like this. Today we will all have a really good think and see if we can find a way to stop Toby worrying.'

33

'Is there a prize?' asked Harry. 'I might think harder if there is a prize.'

'Yes!' I said. 'There's a prize.'

'What is it?' Harry asked.

But just then, the man on the radio said it was ten past eight, so Harry had to rush away before he heard the answer.

★

Dad tried his idea first. He read me my bedtime story, then said, 'If you can go a whole week without calling someone upstairs to look under your bed, I'll buy

you a new bike.'

I was so happy. I lay in bed and thought about my new bike. Would I choose red? Or silver? Maybe even black?

Then I got scared. I tried my hardest not to call them. But in the end, I cracked. 'Da-ad! Mu-um! Na-na! Har-ry!'

The next night, up came Mum. She had her own idea. She dragged every last thing out from under the bed and moved it into the cupboard. Everything! Even the chocolate rabbit I was saving for a special day.

'There!' she said. 'Now you can just lean over and see quite easily that there is nothing scary and horrible under the bed.'

It didn't work. I was too scared to look. I lay there for a while, and then just yelled. 'Da-ad! Mu-um!
Na-na! Har-ry!'

Nana tried next. She came in wearing an old wizard's hat from Halloween.

'I'm going to cast a spell,' she said. 'A Not-To-Worry spell. After I say the words, you'll never, ever worry again about anything under your bed.'

She pointed her finger at me and chanted:

'I heard it from the Sleep-Well Fairy,
    Under your bed there's
        nothing scary.'

I don't think Nana can have passed her wizard exams. It didn't work. Only a few minutes after she'd gone, I heard myself shouting again. 'Da-ad! Mu-um! Na-na! Har-ry!'

Nobody came. I yelled again. I was quite sure I could hear something slithering. I knew I could hear teeth.

Finally, Harry came up. 'I'm dead fed up with this!' he told me. 'I was watching something really good on telly.'

'I'm sorry!' I told him.

'You know you're being stupid?'

'I know! I know!' I felt like crying. 'I just wish there was no such place as under the bed!'

Harry stood staring at me. I could tell that he was thinking hard. And then he said, 'No such place as under the bed? That's brilliant, Toby!'

I hadn't got the faintest idea what
he was on about.

'Come on!' he told me. 'Get out of
bed and help me turn it over.'

'Turn the bed over?' I said. 'Why do
you want to do that?'

'You'll see,' said Harry.

So I got out of bed. We pulled
the duvet and my sheet and pillow on to
the floor. Then we slid off the mattress.
After that, we each took an end of the
bed and turned it upside down.

Harry began to unscrew one of the legs.

'Don't just stand gawping,' he told me. 'Lend a hand. Unscrew that leg over there.'

I did what I was told. He took the third leg off, and I unscrewed the last.

'Right,' Harry said. 'Now help me turn the bed back over.'

We did that, and then we slid the mattress on again. Harry flapped on the bottom sheet and I did all the edges. Then Harry threw on the duvet and I put back the pillow.

'There you go,' Harry said. 'There can't be anything scary and horrible under the bed, because you don't have an under-the-bed any more. So go to sleep!'

Harry went back downstairs to finish watching whatever it was on telly. And I got back into my bed.

It felt so wonderful. I was asleep in minutes.

Harry and I shared the prize. It was
the chocolate rabbit I was saving for
a special day. (It was a special night,
really, but Harry didn't mind. Neither
did I.)

I'd said the brilliant words that set off
Harry's even more brilliant idea, so I
ate the front end of the rabbit,
and Harry ate the
back end.

Now I sleep every
night. We were quite
right. If you don't have
an under-the-bed at all,
there can't be anything
scary under it.

(Not that there ever was.)